Sterling and the CANARY

Andy Stanton

With illustrations by
Ross Collins

Barrington Stoke

Chapter 1
The New Girl

Sterling Thaxton was the best-looking boy in the school. He was tall and strong and everyone was impressed by him, even the teachers. And he was amazing at sports. He could kick a football so high that when it came back down it had a sun-tan. He could smash a tennis ball so far that it could win a tennis match in a different town. He could run faster than all the other kids, even if they were on bikes. And all the girls at school were in love with him. Every single one.

One day a new girl turned up at school, like new girls sometimes do. One day they're not there at all. Then the next day – BINGO! – they just pop up like they've been there all along. As soon as he saw the new girl standing there like she'd been there all along, Sterling Thaxton was in love.

"Look at that girl," he said. "Her hair is the colour of magic. Her nose is as sweet as music. Her arms are as wonderful as rainbows. I want her to be my girlfriend. I would like to hold her hand. I don't mean I

want to chop her hand off and hold it. That would be horrible. But I would like to hold her hand while it was still connected to the rest of her."

"Why don't you go and ask her out?" said Doctor Edward Macintosh.

Doctor Edward Macintosh had long brown hair and a pretty face hidden by thick round glasses. She was Sterling's best friend.

But before we go any further, I'm sure you'd like to know why Doctor Edward Macintosh had such a strange name ...

The Story of Why

Doctor Edward Macintosh

Had Such a Strange Name

When Doctor Edward Macintosh was about to be born, her mum said, "I'm going to close my eyes. Then, when I open them I will name my baby after the first thing I see."

So she closed her eyes.

Then she opened them and she saw a kind-looking man in a long white coat.

"Hello," he smiled. "I am Doctor Edward Macintosh. I'll be looking after you here in the hospital."

And that's how Doctor Edward Macintosh ended up being called Doctor Edward Macintosh.

... Back in the playground, Sterling was still staring at the new girl like he was in a wonderful dream.

"Go on, Sterling," said Doctor Edward Macintosh. "Ask her out. I'm sure she'll say yes. All the girls say yes to you."

"OK," said Sterling. He took a deep breath. He brushed back his blond hair. He drew an arrow on his school shirt pointing to his strong arms.

"LOOK AT MY BIG STRONG ARMS," said the arrow.

Then he walked over to the new girl.

"Hello," said Sterling. "What's your name?"

"Lizzie Harris," said the new girl. Up close, she was even prettier. She was so pretty that Sterling thought his heart might explode out of his chest and try to kiss her.

"That's a nice name," said Sterling. "I'm Sterling Thaxton. Will you go out with me?"

"Let's see," said Lizzie. "You're very good-looking."

"It's true," said Sterling with a grin.

"And I bet you're good at sports, aren't you?"

"Oh, yes," said Sterling happily. "You should see me kick a football – it's an amazing sight."

"And I bet all the girls are in love with you, aren't they?" said Lizzie.

"Oh, yes," said Sterling. "They are."

"Well, not me," said Lizzie. "I don't care how good-looking you are or how good at sports you are or how many girls are in love with you. The only thing I care about is maths."

"But I'm rubbish at maths," said Sterling. "Every time I look at my sums I get so confused I want to scream."

"Well! Don't bother talking to me then," said Lizzie. With a flick of her long brown hair, she turned and walked away.

And Sterling was left standing there, broken-hearted in the rain. I forgot to mention it was raining, but it was. It always rains when you get your heart broken. That's just the law.

Chapter 2
Sterling Does Sums

That evening, Sterling was round at Doctor Edward Macintosh's house. They were watching a film called "Harry the Giant and the Gang of Trees". It was a brilliant film. It was all about a giant called Harry who keeps knocking down trees to use them as pencils. The trees get so sick of Harry the Giant that they gang up on him and turn him into a fridge.

"Turn it off," said Sterling after a while.

"What do you mean?" said Doctor Edward Macintosh. "This is the best bit. This is the bit where all the trees gang up on Harry."

"I'm not in the mood," said Sterling. "All I can think about is Lizzie Harris. I like the way she walks. I like the way she talks. I like the way she sits on a big box full of potatoes under the sea."

"You've never seen her sitting on a box of potatoes under the sea," said Doctor Edward Macintosh.

"That's true," said Sterling. "But I like everything she does. I can't help it."

"You're in love," said Doctor Edward Macintosh. "But don't worry. I'm good at maths. I can teach you maths so you'll be as good as me. Then Lizzie Harris will have to go out with you."

So Doctor Edward Macintosh sat Sterling down at her desk and started asking him sums.

"OK, Sterling. What's two plus three?"

"Um ... A thousand?" said Sterling.

"Not quite," said Doctor Edward Macintosh kindly. "Let's try again. Here, I'll show you how."

At that moment the door flew open and in came Doctor Edward Macintosh's mum.

"How many times do I have to tell you two?" she said. "Stop watching that stupid film about a giant and do your homework instead."

Then she saw what was going on. The TV was off. The children were sitting at the desk, working quietly.

"Oh," said Doctor Edward Macintosh's mum. She shook her head in amazement. "You *are* doing your homework. Sorry. Bye."

For the rest of the evening, Doctor Edward Macintosh and Sterling did sums together.

"What's ten take away five?" said Doctor Edward Macintosh.

"A thousand?" said Sterling.

"Good try," said Doctor Edward Macintosh. "OK, what's six times two?"

"A thousand?" said Sterling.

"Not quite," said Doctor Edward Macintosh. "All right, if I've got one apple in my left hand and two apples in my right hand, how many apples have I got altogether?"

"A thousand?" said Sterling.

"Oh, dear," said Doctor Edward Macintosh. "Right, one last try. What's nine hundred and ninety-nine plus one?"

"Seven?" said Sterling.

"Oh, dear," said Doctor Edward Macintosh. "Shall we have one more go?"

"NO!" shouted Sterling. His face was red. He felt embarrassed about being so bad at maths in front of his best friend. "I'll never be any good at maths!" he shouted. "I don't want your stupid help! Forget it! Goodbye!"

And with that he stormed out of Doctor Edward Macintosh's room, stormed down the stairs, stormed through the front hall and stormed out of the house. Altogether, it was a lot of storming.

"Oh, dear," said Doctor Edward Macintosh. "I was only trying to help."

Chapter 3
The Canary

The next few days were terrible for Sterling.
He still felt embarrassed about being rubbish
at maths. He was upset that he'd been so
angry with Doctor Edward Macintosh. And he
was sad that Lizzie Harris didn't want to go
out with him.

Why didn't he go and say sorry to Doctor
Edward Macintosh? Well, sometimes when

you've done a silly thing it is hard to undo it. You feel so silly about it. And you feel it would be better if you acted as if it hadn't happened at all.

So Sterling didn't say sorry to his best friend. Instead, whenever he saw her in the playground or in a lesson, he just went red and wouldn't look at her.

One evening, Sterling stayed late at school to practise with the football team. Sterling normally scored about ten goals a match, but tonight he hadn't scored any because he was so sad.

"I'm not even any good at football any more," he said as he walked home after the game. "I'm as useless as a broken carrot."

Golden brown leaves lay in deep piles on the ground. The street lamps made puddles of soft yellow light on the pavement. It was one of those magical autumn evenings, all cosy and breezy. But Sterling was too upset to care.

"Stupid football!" he said. "Stupid maths! Stupid Doctor Edward Macintosh! Stupid Lizzie Harris! Stupid leaves!"

Sterling kicked at a big pile of leaves. The leaves went flying everywhere.

"Hey!" came a voice. "What do you think you're doing?"

Sterling looked around. There was no one there. Then he looked down. A little yellow bird was poking its face out of the leaves on the ground. It was a canary. A canary with a little bell around its neck.

"What do think you're doing?" said the canary again. "You nearly kicked my beak off!"

"A talking canary?" said Sterling, bending down. "That's stupid!"

"Oh, is it?" said the canary, puffing out its little yellow chest. "Well, we canaries think it's stupid when we see you humans flying about in aeroplanes too."

"Hmm," said Sterling. "I hadn't thought of that. You're quite a clever canary, aren't you?"

"Yes," said the canary. "I've been to Canary University. I was the best at maths there."

"Well, it was nice to meet you," said Sterling. "Goodbye."

Sterling started walking down the road. Then he stopped.

"Hold on a minute," he said. He ran back to the canary.

"Did you say you were good at maths?" said Sterling.

"Yes," said the canary. "So what?"

"What's six times six?" said Sterling.

"Easy," said the canary. "Thirty-six."

Sterling took out his maths book from his bag. It was a big red book and it was full of sums. It was called "The Big Red Book Of Sums That Sterling Will Never Be Good At".

He looked through the pages.

"You're right!" said Sterling. "Six times six is thirty-six! OK, what's fifty divided by two?"

"Easy," said the canary. "Twenty-five."

"Right again!" said Sterling. "One hundred and seven take away fourteen?"

"Ninety-three," said the canary.

"Thirty plus eight?"

"Thirty-eight," said the canary.

"Nine thousand divided by six?"

"One thousand five hundred," said the canary with a yawn. "Haven't you got anything harder?"

"You're not just good at maths," said Sterling. "You're amazing! Listen, I've got a problem and I wonder if you could lend a hand. I mean, a wing."

The canary thought about it for a bit.

"OK," it said. "It's your lucky day. I'll help you out – but just this once. Don't go expecting it all the time."

So Sterling picked up the canary and put it in his shirt pocket. And he smiled all the way home.

Chapter 4
Sterling Talks to Lizzie Harris

The next day, Sterling was still smiling. He smiled all through Assembly. He smiled all through his lessons. When Doctor Edward Macintosh smiled at him in History, he even smiled back. He couldn't wait for morning break.

At last it came. Sterling rushed out into the playground and saw Doctor Edward Macintosh standing by the wall. She was licking a big fat ice-cream in a cone. Sterling thought about talking to her but then he changed his mind. He had more important things to do.

Lizzie Harris was over by the gates, reading a magazine about film stars and lipstick and fashion. Her hair was the colour of magic. Her nose was as sweet as music. Her arms were as wonderful as rainbows.

Sterling took a deep breath.

He put on a red baseball cap.

"Ready?" said Sterling.

"Ready," whispered the canary from under the baseball cap.

Sterling walked over to Lizzie Harris.

"Hello," said Sterling.

Lizzie Harris was reading a page in her magazine called "Ten Top Tips For Perfect Hair".

She didn't even look up at Sterling.

"I told you, I don't want to talk to you," she said.

"But I'm really good at maths now," said Sterling. "I've been ... er ... I've been practising my sums."

"Oh, really?" said Lizzie Harris, looking up at last. "Well, tell me this. What's thirty plus forty?"

"Seventy," whispered the canary under the baseball cap.

"Seventy," said Sterling.

"Not bad," said Lizzie Harris. "Twenty divided by four?"

"Five," whispered the canary.

"Five," said Sterling.

"Nineteen plus seventy-eight," said Lizzie Harris.

"Ninety-seven," whispered the canary.

"Ninety-seven," said Sterling.

"So you can do maths after all," said Lizzie Harris. "I'm impressed."

"So you'll go out with me then?" said Sterling.

"No, of course not," said Lizzie Harris.

"Great," said Sterling happily. "Shall we go to see a film – hey, hold on a minute! What did you say?"

"I said I'm not going out with you," said Lizzie. "I've changed my mind. I'm not into maths any more."

"What?" said Sterling. He couldn't believe what he was hearing.

"The thing I'm into now is capital cities," said Lizzie Harris. "Are you any good at capital cities, Sterling?"

"No," said Sterling. "I can never remember them. I get them all mixed up."

"What a shame," said Lizzie Harris. "You'd better not bother talking to me then."

Lizzie Harris flipped over her magazine and started reading a page called "Ten Ways To Break A Boy's Heart".

It had started to rain again. Sterling turned and walked away through the wet playground.

"Are you OK, Sterling?" said Doctor Edward Macintosh.

"Not really," said Sterling.

"I heard what she said," said Doctor Edward Macintosh. "You know, I could help you learn your capital cities."

"I don't want your help," said Sterling. "It's all gone wrong. Leave me alone."

And he ran back into the school. His eyes were wet. But he told himself he wasn't crying – it must have just been the rain.

Chapter 5
Capital Cities

Sterling was in his bedroom. He was sulking. The canary hopped about on his bed, eating the bird-seed that Sterling had put out on his pillow. The little bell round its neck rang when it hopped.

"It's all right for you," said Sterling. "All you do is flap around and eat. You haven't ever had your heart broken."

The canary didn't reply. It just bent down and pecked up another bit of bird-seed with its beak.

"Stupid canary," said Sterling. "Why did I ever trust you?"

He turned back to the book on his desk. It was called "Capital Cities Of The World That Sterling Will Never Be Able To Remember".

He sighed.

Then the phone rang. Sterling picked it up.

"Hello?" he said. For one crazy second, he thought it might be Lizzie Harris, even though she didn't have his number.

"Hello, Sterling," said the voice down the line. It was Doctor Edward Macintosh. "I just thought I'd see how you are."

"I'm fine," said Sterling. He wasn't really. He was lying. "I've never been better."

"OK," said Doctor Edward Macintosh. "But listen. If you do need any help with those capital cities, I'm your girl."

"Well, I don't," said Sterling. His face was all red and he felt embarrassed. He was glad his friend couldn't see him. "I'm *fine*, all right?"

"All right," said Doctor Edward Macintosh. Then she said, "Look, you're my best friend and I want you to be happy. Are you sure that going out with Lizzie Harris is what you really want?"

"Of course it is," said Sterling.

"And you're sure you won't let me help?"

"I told you, I don't need your help," said Sterling. "Good *bye!*"

Sterling slammed down the phone. He felt stupid.

'Maybe I should phone back and say sorry,' he thought. But no. He couldn't do it. It would make him feel even more stupid.

"I'm so confused!" he said out loud. "I don't know what to do any more. And I'll never remember all those stupid capital cities!"

"Did you say capital cities?" said the canary suddenly, looking up from the bed.

"Yeah," said Sterling. "So what?"

The canary pecked at another bit of bird-seed. Then it looked back at Sterling.

"It just so happens that I am brilliant at capital cities," said the canary. "I learned all about capital cities at Canary University."

"I thought you said you did maths at Canary University," said Sterling.

"Boy, you really are stupid," said the canary. "You don't have to just do one thing at Canary University. Even a sparrow knows that. I did maths *and* capital cities. And, as a matter of fact, I came top of the class. I know every capital city in the world."

"Oh," said Sterling, feeling quite foolish. "I'm sorry. So will you help me then?"

The canary thought about it for a bit.

"OK," it said. "Seeing as I'm in a good mood I'll help you out again."

Chapter 6
A Boring Weekend

For once in his life, Sterling couldn't wait
to get back to school. But the next day was
Saturday, so he had to wait. And do you
know what made it worse? Normally on a
Saturday he would go over to Doctor Edward
Macintosh's house and they would play all
sorts of games. Sometimes they would play
on the computer. Sometimes they would play
in the park. And sometimes they would play a

chase game they had made up called "Marshy and Greedy Pig".

Marshy and Greedy Pig was the best game ever. One person was Marshy and one person was Greedy Pig. Greedy Pig would chase Marshy around and around the table in the front room. But just when Greedy Pig was about to catch Marshy, Marshy would shout out:

"Marshy in the dark! Marshy in the dark!"

And then you had to turn the lights off and the chase would carry on in the dark, with lots of bashing into the table and giggling.

One time they had started giggling so much they couldn't stop and they thought they were going to be sick.

But this Saturday there was no chance of going over to Doctor Edward Macintosh's house. And no chance of playing Marshy and Greedy Pig.

Sterling let out a big long sigh. He tried to imagine playing Marshy and Greedy Pig with Lizzie Harris. But somehow he couldn't see it. Somehow he thought Lizzie Harris wasn't the kind of person who would enjoy playing Marshy and Greedy Pig.

"Never mind," said Sterling to himself. "Once Lizzie Harris is my girlfriend I won't need silly things like Marshy and Greedy Pig anyway. That's just for babies."

Sterling made himself a sandwich for lunch. He put too much mustard in. It was revolting. After lunch he sat around throwing balls of paper into the bin.

"You look bored," said Sterling's mum. "Why don't you go and see Doctor Edward Macintosh?"

"Don't feel like it," said Sterling.

"But she's your best friend," said Sterling's mum.

"Don't care," said Sterling. "Don't feel like it."

Sterling's mum gave up on the subject. "One other thing," she said. "Why is there bird poo all over your bedroom floor?"

"Dunno," said Sterling.

Sterling's mum gave up on that subject too.

Sunday was even worse than Saturday. Sterling just flopped around the house like a bored pancake. In the end, Sterling's mum couldn't stand it any more.

"I'm not having you lying around here all day," she said. "Go out and get some fresh air in your lungs."

So Sterling went down to the park. Sometimes he and Doctor Edward Macintosh would go to the park and pretend to be detectives. They would pretend the other people in the park were crime suspects.

One Saturday, they had watched an old man sitting on a bench for ages. When he got up they followed him and said things like, "The suspect is now walking past the tennis courts."

"The suspect has now stopped by the duck pond."

"The suspect is now throwing bread to the ducks."

Doctor Edward Macintosh said the old man wasn't throwing bread to the ducks at all. She reckoned the old man was a bank robber. And the bread wasn't bread, it was really secret messages about where the money was hidden.

But today Sterling didn't feel like following any suspects. It wasn't the same on his own. After a while he went back home. He went upstairs to the bathroom. He brushed his teeth and got ready for bed. It was still only seven o'clock. But Sterling wasn't in the mood for anything.

"Never mind," he said as he lay back on the pillow. "Tomorrow's the big day. Tomorrow's the day I get to ask Lizzie Harris out again. And this time she'll say yes."

The canary sat on top of Sterling's computer. It didn't say a word.

Chapter 7
Another Talk with Lizzie Harris

It felt to Sterling that morning break would never come. The lessons seemed to go much slower than normal. It was like someone had set the world to the wrong speed.

"To ... day ... we ... will ... be ... lear-ning ... a ... bout ... the ... Ro ... mans ..." said the History teacher. It seemed like each word lasted about a hundred years.

AAARGGH! Sterling couldn't stand it.

"Come on, come on," he kept saying under his breath.

Doctor Edward Macintosh smiled at Sterling from across the classroom but he didn't even notice. He was too busy looking at the clock.

"The ... Ro ... mans ... were ... very ... inter ... esting," said the teacher. Sterling was sure time had slowed down. Soon time would start going backwards. Maybe it would go backwards all the way to Roman times. Then they wouldn't have to learn about the Romans from some boring History teacher. They could just go up to one of the Romans and ask them instead.

"The ... Ro ... mans ... built ... lots ... of ... very ... inter ... esting ... things," said the teacher.

AAAAAARRRRGH!

"Come on, come on, come on!" said Sterling.

Morning break came around at last. Sterling rushed out into the playground. Doctor Edward Macintosh was standing by the wall. She was eating another big fat ice-cream in a cone. Sterling rushed past her without even saying hello. He looked around. Then he saw Lizzie Harris.

She was by the drinking fountain, putting on make-up.

Her hair was the colour of magic. Her nose was as sweet as music. Her arms were as wonderful as rainbows.

Sterling took out his secret weapon. It was his red baseball cap and I'm sure you know what was hidden inside. He put it on.

"Ready?" he said.

"Ready," whispered the canary.

Sterling walked up to Lizzie Harris.

"Hello again," he said. "It's me – Sterling."

"Big deal," said Lizzie Harris. She wasn't looking at Sterling. She was looking at herself in a mirror while she put on lipstick.

"Yes, but I can do capital cities now," said Sterling. "Really I can."

Lizzie Harris looked up.

"All right, what's the capital of Italy?" she said.

"Rome," whispered the canary inside the baseball cap.

"Rome," said Sterling.

"What's the capital of Russia?" said Lizzie Harris.

"Moscow," whispered the canary.

"Moscow," said Sterling.

"What's the capital of Japan?" said Lizzie Harris.

"Tokyo," whispered the canary.

"Tokyo," said Sterling.

"I'm impressed," said Lizzie Harris. "Did you learn all those capitals just for me?"

"Yes," said Sterling. "So now, I beg you – will you go out with me?"

"No," said Lizzie Harris.

"Fantastic," said Sterling. "I was thinking we could go for a walk in the – hey, what do you mean?"

"I mean no, I won't go out with you," said Lizzie Harris. She was painting a big red smile on her face in lipstick. "I've changed my mind again. I don't care about capital cities."

"What?" said Sterling. He couldn't believe what he was hearing.

"What I care about now is types of flowers," said Lizzie Harris. "Do you know about flowers?"

"No," said Sterling. "They all look the same to me."

Lizzie Harris reached over with her lipstick and drew a big unhappy mouth on Sterling's face.

"Come back when you know about flowers," she said. "Then I'll go out with you."

"No you won't," said Sterling. "You'll just change your mind again."

"No, this time I mean it," said Lizzie Harris. "This time I truly mean it."

Just then the canary whispered something in Sterling's ear.

"Listen, I'm really good at types of flowers too," said the canary. "That was the other thing I did at Canary University. Maths, capital cities and types of flowers."

"That's lucky," said Sterling. "You really are a clever canary."

"Who are you talking to?" said Lizzie Harris. "Are you some sort of freak?"

"No," said Sterling. "But I've just remembered that I am very good at flowers after all. Ask me anything you like."

Chapter 8
Lizzie Harris Says Yes

Lizzie Harris looked at Sterling Thaxton.

"You sure you're ready for this?" she said.

"Yes," said Sterling. "Go on – ask me anything."

"OK," said Lizzie Harris. She pointed to a flower in the flower bed next to the drinking fountain. "What's that one called?"

"Rose," whispered the canary.

"That's a rose," said Sterling.

"Good start," said Lizzie Harris. "What's that one?"

"Buttercup," whispered the canary.

"It's a buttercup, of course," said Sterling.

"And that one?" said Lizzie Harris.

"Daisy," whispered the canary.

"It's a daisy," said Sterling.

"Well done," said Lizzie Harris. "You've passed my third and final test."

"So will you go out with me?" said Sterling.

"Yes," said Lizzie Harris.

"Oh, dear," said Sterling. "I knew you'd change your mind again – hang on, what did you say?"

"I said, yes, I'll go out with you," said Lizzie Harris.

"Wow!" smiled Sterling. He could hardly believe what he was hearing.

"You can start by taking me out to a posh restaurant," said Lizzie Harris. "Then I want you to take me shopping. I want a new dress. I want a gold necklace. I want new shoes. Then you can take me dancing so everyone can see how nice I look."

Sterling looked at Lizzie Harris. He didn't know what to say.

"You do think I look nice, don't you?" said Lizzie Harris.

Sterling looked at Lizzie Harris again.

He thought about all the trouble she'd put him through.

He thought about how she kept changing her mind.

He thought about all the things she wanted.

Suddenly he wasn't sure she looked so nice after all.

He looked over at Doctor Edward Macintosh, standing by the wall with her ice-cream cone.

He thought about how she was always there to help him.

He thought about playing Marshy and Greedy Pig.

And he'd never really noticed before but she had a lovely smile.

"Sorry," said Sterling to Lizzie Harris. "Maybe another time."

"What?" said Lizzie Harris. She could hardly believe what she was hearing. "No one says no to Lizzie Harris! No one!"

But Sterling was already walking away.

He walked up to Doctor Edward Macintosh.

"I'm sorry I've been such an idiot lately," said Sterling. "I don't think that girl's right for me at all."

"Are you sure?" said Doctor Edward Macintosh.

"I'm sure," said Sterling. He took a deep breath. "Doctor Edward Macintosh. Will you go out with me?"

"What, as friends?" said Doctor Edward Macintosh.

"Well, yes," said Sterling. "But I was wondering if you would like to be my girlfriend too."

"I'd love to," said Doctor Edward Macintosh.

Sterling took off his baseball cap and the canary flew out and chirped around his head. The little bell around its neck fell off and rolled away.

In fact, it wasn't a bell at all.

It was a tiny metal speaker that sounds could come out of.

While Sterling wasn't looking, Doctor Edward Macintosh put her ice-cream cone away in her bag.

In fact, it wasn't an ice-cream cone at all.

It was a microphone.

So you see, Doctor Edward Macintosh had been trying to help Sterling out all along. But all the same, she was glad he hadn't chosen Lizzie Harris.

Sterling put out his hand and Doctor Edward Macintosh took it. And together they walked along the playground, hand in hand.

It was funny, but the canary never did talk again after that. But Sterling didn't mind. He was holding his best friend's hand and the sun was shining and he was in love.

Our books are tested
for children and young people by
children and young people.

Thanks to everyone who consulted on
a manuscript for their time and effort in
helping us to make our books better
for our readers.

Interview
with
Andy STANTON!

Was it hard to write *Sterling and the Canary*? Did you have to make many changes?

It's always easier to write a book when you get a good idea. I had the idea of a boy who finds a talking canary. And after that, the rest of the story followed without too much trouble. But I had to make a few changes as I went along. When I first wrote the story, Doctor Edward Macintosh was a boy. Then I decided it would be good for Sterling to have a nice girl in his life, so I changed her into a girl. At first she wasn't called Doctor Edward Macintosh. She was called Hospital Wall! But in the end, I thought Hospital Wall was too crazy a name – even for me.

What is your favourite capital city?

Well, I'd probably have to say London because I live there. I don't think I've been to many other capital cities. Paris is nice but I'm rubbish at French. I'd need a canary who could speak French to help me out if I lived in Paris.

Can you tell us a secret not many people know?

Marshy and Greedy Pig is a real game! I used to play it with my little brother and it's the funniest game ever. There are some other rules that I didn't put in the story because there wasn't room. But really it's just very silly and lots of fun. You have to sing "Greedy, greedy, greedy, greedy! Greedy Pig!" over and over while you're playing it.

What was your favourite book when you were young?

The Eighteenth Emergency by Betsy Byars. It's a really great story about a boy called Mouse who's been cheeky to the school bully. The whole book is about how worried he is that he'll get beaten up. The story is sad and funny all at the same time. I can still remember getting it out from the library when I was 8. I took it home and read it at the kitchen table. I couldn't stop reading, it was so good. Go and read it NOW!

Do you like animals?

I think animals are the funniest things in the world. Especially cats. But I am a bit of a wimp. I'm scared of most animals. I'm from the city so I don't really know what to do with a cow or a horse or a pig. Mostly I just run away.

Will there be a canary - or a puffin or a kingfisher or a condor or a macaw - in your next book?

I don't know! I never know what my next idea will be. But I do think that the word "eagle" is very funny. Say it over and over – "Eagle!" "Eagle!" "Eagle!" "Eagle!" "Eagle!" Words sound so weird when you say them again and again. Try it with some different words. It's so strange.

When you were at school did you like Maths or Sports best?

I wasn't brilliant at Maths. I was just OK. And I wasn't brilliant at Sports either, so it's a hard choice. I quite liked both subjects but I preferred English.

Would you like to go to Canary University?

Yes, it sounds brilliant. Much better than Oxford University. I went there but they kicked me out! I hate them!